This book belongs to

....

Written by Rosie Greening.
Illustrated by Kali Stileman.

No Probllama!

Rosie Greening • Kali Stileman

make
believe
ideas

Llama loved to **boast**. "I'm **faster** than **YOU**," he told Cheetah.

LL4M4

"I could grow a better mane than **YOURS**, Lion."

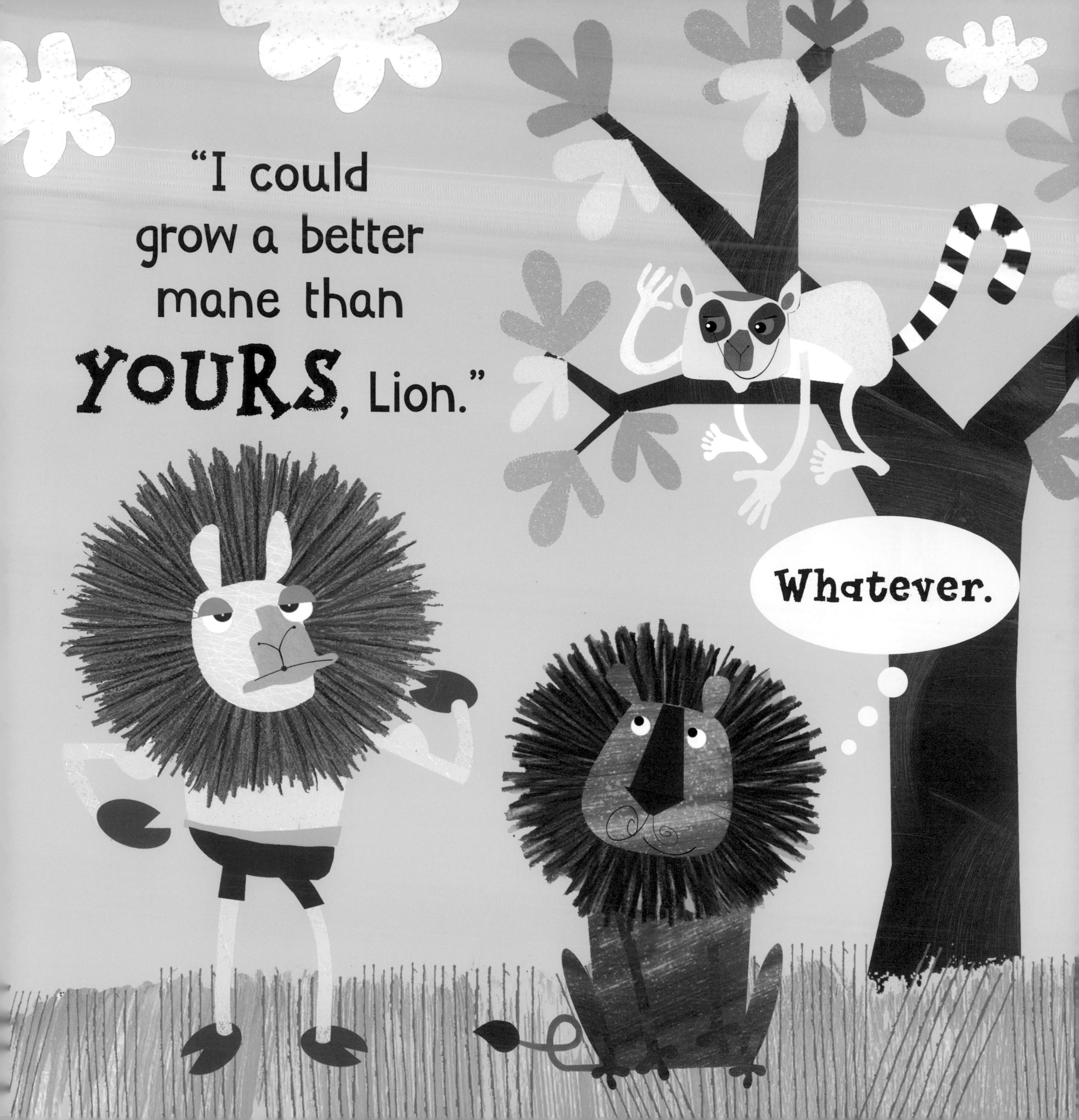

Every day, Lemur watched on and tried to **ignore** Llama.

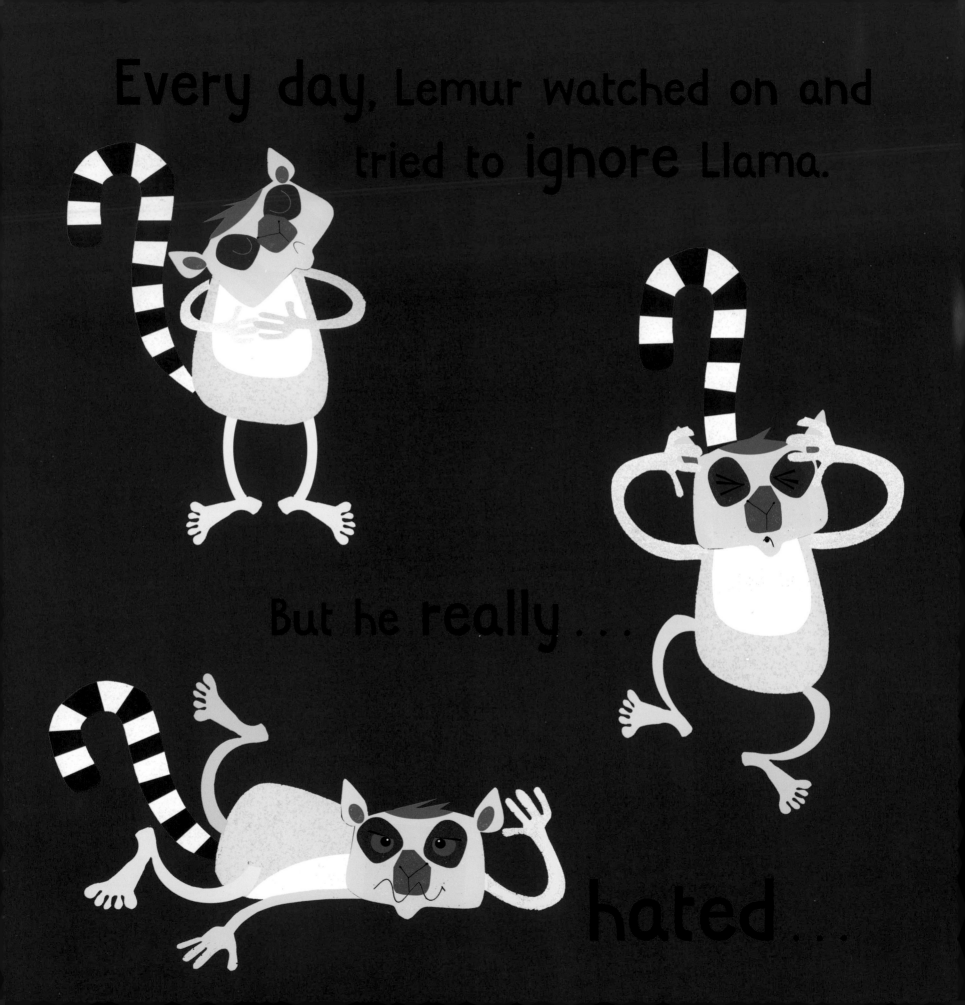

But he **really** . . .

hated . . .

One morning, Lemur decided to put Llama to the **test**.

"Oi, Llama!" he shouted.

"Can you **paint?**"

"Can you do **karate?**"

"Can you talk
underwater?"

"No prob-bllub-bllub-bllama!"

"Can you SING...

whilst standing
on your head?"

"Can you swing like a monkey?"

"Can you drink tea on a surfboard?"

"Can you do **ballet**...

on a
mountain...

...in a **snowstorm?**"

"No probrrr brrrrrrr-llama!"

"Can you skydive?"

"Do you
know how
to get
home?"

"No probLEMUR!"

"Oh dear."

SOS